TROTTER STREET is a street in a community in England. It could be anywhere—London, Cambridge, or Blackpool. For this reason, the text is exactly as it appears in the British edition. There are a few words that may need translation for American children: A "flat" is an apartment; a "lift" is an elevator; a baby's "cot" is a crib.

First U.S. edition 1 2 3 4 5 6 7 8 9 10

Library of Congress Cataloging-in-Publication Data
Hughes, Shirley. Angel Mae: a tale of Trotter Street.
Summary: The Christmas season at Mae's house is enlivened by the arrival of a new baby and Mae's appearance in a Christmas play. [1. Babies—Fiction. 2. Christmas—Fiction. 3. Plays—Fiction] I. Title. PZ7.H87395Amo 1989 [E] 89-45288
ISBN 0-688-08538-5 ISBN 0-688-08539-3 (lib. bdg.)

Printed in Italy.

A Tale of Trotter Street

Angel Mae

Shirley Hughes

Lothrop, Lee & Shepard Books
New York

Mae Morgan lived with her mum and dad and her big brother Frankie in the flats on the corner of Trotter Street. Mae's grandma lived nearby. Soon there was going to be another person in the family, because Mae's mum was going to have a baby. It would be born around Christmas time.

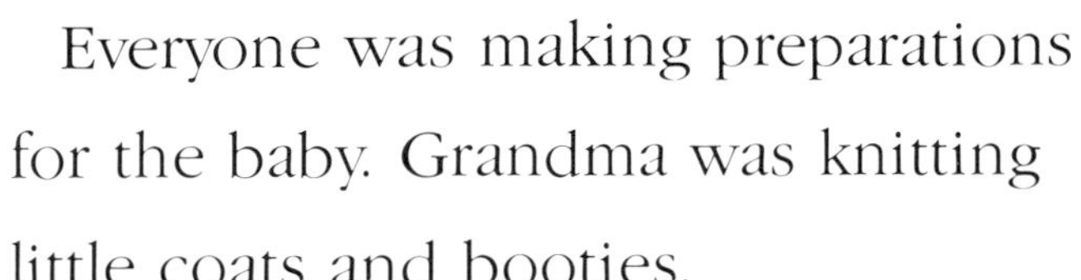

Everyone was making preparations for the baby. Grandma was knitting little coats and booties.

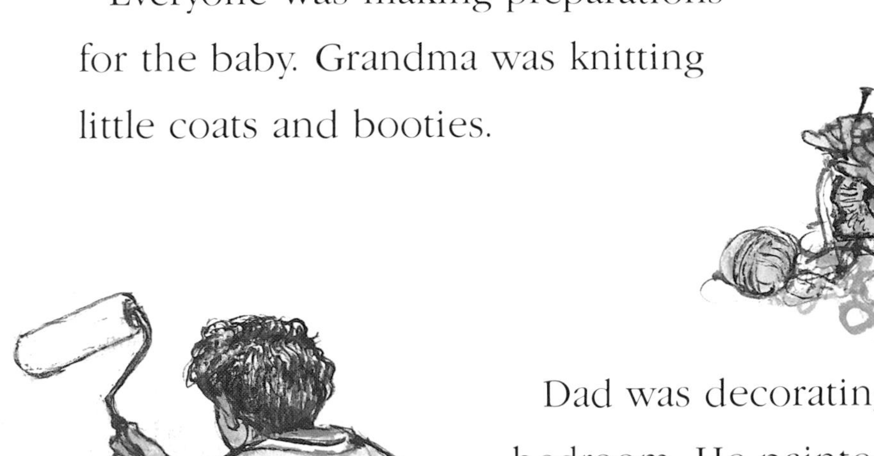

Dad was decorating the small bedroom. He painted the walls a beautiful yellow.

Mum got out the old cradle that Mae and Frankie had slept in when they were babies. She put a pretty new lining in it.

"Imagine us being small enough to sleep in that!" said Frankie.

Mae tried sitting in the cradle. She could just fit if her knees were drawn up under her chin.

Mae thought about the baby a lot. She looked into her toy chest and pulled out some of her old toys. She was hoping to have some lovely new things at Christmas, so she thought she would give the baby a few of her old toys.

She didn't want to give away anything too special, like her best doll, Carol. She thought she could let the baby have her old pink rabbit and the duck who nodded his head and flapped his wings when you pulled him along. And there was the ball with the bell inside it. They were all too babyish for her now.

Carefully, Mae put the rabbit, the duck and the ball into the baby's cradle.

"What are you putting those old toys in there for?" asked Frankie. "Our new baby will be much too small to play with those." And he told Mae that at first it would be a tiny little baby, not nearly big enough to play with toys. "But he might like them when he's older," Frankie said.

"How do you know it will be a he?" Mae answered crossly.

Frankie said he didn't know, but he hoped it would be so he could teach the baby to play football.

Mae slowly piled up her old toys and threw them on the floor beside her toy chest.

The flat where Mae and Frankie lived was on the third floor. There were a good many stairs because there wasn't a lift. Mum got tired carrying up the shopping.

Mae got tired too. She wished she could be carried like a shopping bag.

"Carry me, carry me," she moaned, drooping on the banisters at the bottom step. But Mum couldn't carry Mae *and* the shopping. Mae was much too old to be carried anyway.

After lunch Mum sat down for a rest. Frankie put a cushion under her poor tired feet. Mae moped about. She counted Mum's toes — one, two, three, four — up to ten. Then she started to tickle her feet. But Mum didn't want her feet tickled just then. She lay back and closed her eyes, but Mae knew she wasn't really asleep.

Mae went off to find Dad. He was getting ready to clean the car. He said that Mae could help if she liked, so together they went downstairs into the street.

Dad gave Mae a rag so she could polish the hubcaps. Mae rubbed away until she could see her own face. It looked a bit funny.

"Do you think our baby will be a boy or a girl?" she asked.

"Nobody knows for sure," said Dad. "But as there's you and Mum and Grandma in our family already, it would even things up if it was a boy, wouldn't it?" He ruffled Mae's hair. "You'd like to have a baby brother, wouldn't you, Mae?"

But Mae said nothing. She just went on polishing.

At school, all the children were getting ready for Christmas. Mae's teacher, Mrs Foster, helped them to make paper robins and lanterns to decorate the classroom. Then Mrs Foster told everybody that they were going to act a play about baby Jesus being born. All the Trotter Street mums and dads would be invited to watch.

Nancy Jones was going to be Mary and wear a blue hood over her long fair hair,

and Jim Zolinski was going to be Joseph and wear a false beard.

Frankie, Harvey and Billy were going to be kings. They had gold paper crowns with jewels painted round them.

Mae wanted to be a king too, but Mrs Foster said that kings were boys' parts. Mae looked into the wooden box which Mrs Foster had made into a manger for the baby Jesus.

"I'll be baby Jesus, then," said Mae. She was sure she could fit into the manger if she tried very hard.

But Mrs Foster explained that they were going to wrap up a baby doll in a shawl to be baby Jesus. She said that Mae could be a cow or a sheep if she liked, but Mae certainly didn't want to be either of those. She stuck out her bottom lip and made a very cross face.

"What about being an angel?" asked Mrs Foster.

Mae didn't want to be an angel either.

"You could be the angel Gabriel," Mrs Foster told her. "That's a very special angel, a very important part."

Mae thought about this. Then she nodded her head.

"I'm going to be the angel Gave-you!" she told Frankie later.

"Angel who?" said Frankie.

"Angel Gave-you! A very special angel," said Mae proudly.

"I'm the angel Gave-you!" Mae announced, beaming, when Mum came to collect her.

"Gave-you, Gave-you, Gave-you!" sang Mae as she bounced along ahead, all the way home.

"Angel Gave-you!" shouted Mae, hugging Dad round the waist when he came home from work.

"Gave me what?" asked Dad.

"Just Gave-you. That's my name in the Christmas play," Mae explained.

"Will you come and see us in it?" Frankie wanted to know.

Dad said he wasn't sure, but he would try very hard.

But when Mae and Frankie woke up on the morning of the Christmas play, neither Mum nor Dad was there! Grandma was cooking breakfast. She told them that Dad had taken Mum to the hospital in the night because the new baby was going to be born very soon.

"Will they be back in time to watch me being the angel Gave-you?" asked Mae anxiously.

"I'm afraid not," said Grandma. "But I'll be there for sure."

When Mae and Frankie arrived at school, the big hall looked very different. There was a blue curtain at one end with silver stars all over it and one big star hanging up in the middle. The smallest angels were going to stand on a row of chairs at the back. The animals were going to crouch down in front by the manger.

While the grown-ups were arriving, Mrs Foster helped the children to dress up. Mae had a white pillowcase over her front and a pair of white paper wings pinned on to the back. She was going to stand at the very end of the row because she was such a special angel.

From high up she could see all round the room. She could see all the mums and dads. Grandma was sitting in the very front row, smiling and smiling. Then Mrs Foster sat down at the piano and all the children began to sing:

"Away in a manger, no crib for a bed,
The little Lord Jesus lay down his sweet head..."

Mary and Joseph sang, the angels sang and the animals sang. The shepherds came in and knelt down on one side of the manger. Then the three kings came in, carrying presents for baby Jesus.

Mae sang very loudly.

Then she saw somebody coming in late at the very back of the room. It was Dad! He was smiling the biggest smile of all. Mae was so pleased to see him that she forgot she was in a play. She waved and shouted out, "Hello, Dad. I'm being the angel Gave-you!"

Dad put his fingers to his lips and waved back.

But Mae was waving so hard
that her chair began to wobble...

and Mae wobbled too...

and then she fell
right off the chair...

Bump!

She hit the floor
with a horrible crash,
wings and all!

Mrs Foster stopped playing the piano. All the children stopped singing. Everyone looked at Mae.

Mae held her arm where it hurt. She stuck out her bottom lip. She wanted to cry. But she didn't. Instead, she climbed up on to the chair again and went on singing:

"The stars in the bright sky
looked down where he lay,
The little Lord Jesus
asleep in the hay..."

Then all the people in the audience smiled and clapped a special clap for Mae for being so brave and not spoiling the play. Grandma clapped harder than anyone.

"Good old angel Gave-you!" said Dad when it was all over.

Grandma gave Frankie and Mae a hug and said it was the best Christmas play she had ever seen.

Then Dad said he had a big surprise for them. They had a new baby sister, born that morning. And Mum was going to bring her home in time for Christmas!

When Mae and Frankie went to the hospital, they looked into the cot and saw their tiny baby sister wrapped up in a white shawl. She had a funny little, crumpled up, red face and a few spikes of hair standing on end, and tiny crumpled up fingers. Mae liked the way she looked and she liked her nice baby smell. She was pleased that the baby looked so funny.

But most of all she was pleased that Mum would be home in time for Christmas.